Crazy and In Love with a Georgia Kingpin

A Novella By

M 'Chelle

Unique Creations Publications is now accepting manuscripts from aspiring & experienced authors!

WHAT MAKES YOU UNIQUE

Reaching for your goals no matter who doubts you is what makes you unique. Not letting this world take away your creativity and remaining humble no matter what causes you to stand out. When life gets tough, don't give up; just keep pushing for the stars. The people that shine the brightest are often the ones who have been down the darkest roads.

Legal Notes

DEDICATION

I would like to dedicate my first book to my grandparents;
Rebecca Quinn, Mac Neil and Joe Pearl Coleman. Thanks for always
being a great example of achieving ones hopes and dreams inspite of.

Acknowledgments

I would like to thank everyone who has believed in me and encouraged me through this process. My parents, siblings, and friends. The entire Quinn, Coleman, Terrell, and Brown family. To my business partner, Domaneque who inspired me to start writing again. A special thanks to my husband, Andre, I love you and thank you for always encouraging me and reminding me of the bigger picture. Also, a special thanks to my children Alexis, AJ, Tassai, and Denzel; I love you all, thanks for making this thing called life more interesting. My publisher and entire UCP family. Thanks for taking a chance on me.

Synopsis

Kiesha Devereaux is a caramel-colored southern debutante who's always had a desire for the finer things in life and bad boys. Being Noah Devereaux's daughter has taught her how to hold it down in the streets as well as in the professional world. Her streets smart and business sense paired with her killer body makes her irresistible. It was no surprise she caught the eye of Roman Case, a real estate agent by day and a murdering king-pin by night.

Playboy Roman Case has been in the game since a teen and knows the streets of Atlanta like the back of his hands. When he falls in love with Kiesha his whole life changes when her father Noah Devereaux, the drug king-pin turned media mogul hands him the keys to his empire. He tries his best to honor Noah's wishes to treat his daughter like the princess she is but with women at his disposal it's hard to keep that promise. Roman is on top of the world when it starts to crumble when he underestimates his archrival Frantz Louis, head of the Haitian Mob who takes his most prized possession, Kiesha.

How far will Roman go to get the love of his life or will his old playboy habits get in the way? Join Kiesha and Roman as they navigate through the streets of Georgia and find out what it really means to be crazy and in love with a GA kingpin.

Chapter 1

Kiesha stood in front of the mirror trying to see if she could catch a glimpse of her former self. The scars and bruises let her instantly know that she was long gone. Kiesha Devereux was raised a southern debutante and came from old money, her great-great-grandfather was a real estate mogul in the state of Georgia. It was no surprise that someone like Roman Case would catch her eye. He was a dope boy turned kingpin/business owner. It was something about his swagger that had Kiesha intoxicated with lust. Kiesha led a sheltered life until their lives collided, and it was one adventure after another until one day it all changed.

Kiesha looked toward the bed and saw Roman stirring under the covers of their California King and beside him was Bianca, his new flavor of the week. Although Kiesha hated this she knew Roman has an insatiable appetite. She dealt with it because she was able to drive a 2019 Lexus LS500 and the whole world was at her fingertips. It was nothing to catch a plane to Dubai and party with the crème da la crème. She walked over to the balcony of their beach villa and inhaled the ocean water and felt the sun kiss her beautiful skin.

"Good Morning," he said as he walked outside to join her. The warm breeze and glistening ocean made the day feel perfect, a trip to their beach home was a much-needed getaway from the city. Roman had various properties throughout the state of Georgia but the beach house in Tybee Island was Kiesha's favorite.

He called to Bianca to dismiss herself and informed her a driver was downstairs to take her anywhere she wanted to go. Bianca huffed as she began to get dressed. See you guys later she called out as she left the bedroom. Roman wrapped his muscular arms around Kiesha, she let out a small giggle.

"Good Morning," she said as she gave him a peck on the cheek.

"Last night was amazing and I am starving this morning, can you let Norman know we will be doing breakfast outside this morning." Roman patted her on the bottom as she walked inside to inform the house manager of Roman's request. Roman also walked inside to make one last call to ensure his guest would still be in attendance to his morning meeting.

Kiesha hummed as she took the elevator to see Norman. Norman was an older grey -haired man, he worked with Roman for almost ten years. One afternoon Roman was riding through the streets of Atlanta and saw a couple of guys beating Norman, Roman intervened and the rest was history. Norman was eternally grateful for Roman's generosity and the two adopted a father/son relationship.

"Norman can you have the servants set breakfast up on the lanai per Mr. Case's request," Kiesha said.

"Right away Madam," Norman stated.

Kiesha rode the elevator upstairs and was greeted by Roman with a glass of Cranberry Prosecco. He was fully dressed; he had on a Versace blue baroque shirt with the pants and slippers to match.

"Get dressed," he demanded. Kiesha went into the spacious marbled bathroom to take a quick shower. She put on her fitted Fendi logo dress along with her Fendi strappy heels. She spritzed on YSL perfume. She did a light beat on her face and touched up her bob. She was dressed and ready for whatever Roman had in store.

"Ok, I am looking forward to seeing you," Roman said as he disconnected his cellphone when Kiesha walked onto the lanai. The servants were setting up a buffet of deli meats, cheeses, fresh fruit, and bagels.

"Wow, this is impressive," Kiesha exclaimed.

"We are having a quick business meeting this morning," Roman stated.

"Frantz Louis is here for you Mr. Case," Norman announced. Kiesha shot Roman a confused and evil glare.

"Frantz how are you," Roman said while extending his hand.

"Bonjour," Frantz replied while looking at Kiesha. Kiesha was wondering why in the hell would Roman invite her worst nightmare to breakfast and in her home?

"It's been a long time," Frantz said as he tried to kiss Kiesha's hand. She pulled her hand back in disgust.

"What is this?" she asked Roman.

"Nothing darling just tying up a loose end," Roman said while kissing Kiesha on the forehead. She knew exactly what that meant.

"Have a seat Mr. Louis, my staff has prepared a feast."

"Thanks," he said unbeknownst to the danger that awaited him. Frantz began to fix a plate and devour the meal that was in front of him.

"This is delicious but can we get down to business? I have a busy day."

"Of course," Roman replied.

"A few months ago, we had a slight cash flow problem and for your troubles, you held my most prized possession until I was able to deliver."

Frantz looked at Kiesha and flashed a smile, his disgusting gold teeth glistened.

"Oh yes, I remember," he said with a French accent.

"I have thought about it for months and I would like to repay you for all your kindness through my difficult transition within my company," Roman said.

"Kiesha, can you please bring my briefcase so I can repay Mr. Louis." Frantz kept on eating and rambling on about how important it was to pay your debts on time to avoid unwanted situations. Kiesha opened the briefcase and wielded a .45 with a silencer and pointed it to the back of Frantz's head. Pow, the bullet left the chamber and penetrated Frantz's skull. He fell face-first into his dinner plate. Kiesha wiped the sweat from her forehead and tears began to form. She was shaking, Roman walked over to take the gun out of her hands.

"It's over now," he said while grabbing the gun. "I told you that I wouldn't let him get away with what he did to you."

Kiesha was relieved but also worried about the actions they both had taken.

&&&

A few months ago, Kiesha was shopping at Lenox Square when she noticed Frantz's right-hand man, Samuel following her. She attempted to reach Roman on the cell, but it went straight to voicemail. Kiesha decided to leave the mall and she was met with two more of Frantz's men. One of them pressed a knife to her side and demanded she go with them. She did as she was told, Roman has constantly drilled her on what to do in situations like this. When Kiesha stepped into the van, Frantz was sitting on the back seat.

"Bonjour madame," he said with those ugly ass gold teeth showing. Then he paused without saying anything. He stared me down as he licked his lips. Then he uttered,"Roman has been a busy man, too busy to make his drop. When I employed Roman, he assured me that he had the state of Georgia on lock and it was not going to be an issue when it was time for a payment."

"I don't have anything to do with that," Kiesha said, fighting back tears.

"I know but I expect some sort of collateral until he corrects this problem,"Frantz said while running his hand up Kiesha's dress. He noticed she wasn't wearing underwear and slid his fingers into her tight pussy. She winced from disgust and pain. Kiesha spit in his face and he backhanded her. His ring cut her lip and blood began to drip down her face.

Chapter 2

Kiesha was panicking inside because she was at the mercy of one of the most ruthless men she had ever seen besides Roman.

"I assure you that these next few hours will go smoothly if you cooperate and if you don't it will be very long," said Frantz. Frantz took the cigar from his mouth and burned Kiesha's inner thigh.

"Fuck you, " Kiesha spat venomously. "Roman will kill you when he finds out what you did," she spatted.

Frantz puffed his cigar again and blew the smoke towards her face and let out a chuckle.

"Not only will Roman make his payment but I guarantee he won't touch a hair on my head, this is a what do you Americans say? Misfortune."

Kiesha sat quietly as the van took various twists and turns. It didn't have windows, so she didn't have a clue as to where she was going, she only noticed that the weather began to change, and she was growing colder. They had been riding for a couple of hours and her ears started to pop, she could only assume they were in the mountains. The van came to an abrupt stop, Frantz gave instructions to his men in French.
"L'emmener au sous-sol," he shouted as he stepped out of the van.

Samuel grabbed her by her shoulders and forced her out of the van, the air was cold and crisp, Kiesha was trembling from fear and the cold weather.

"Move your ass," Samuel said in a menacing voice. At first, she did not think they would hurt her but the burn on her inner thigh told a different story. This situation was becoming a little too real and she was terrified. Samuel took her to a dim lit room that was damp and smelled of musk and mold. There was a small bed in the middle of the room, blood stained the walls and there were urine stains on the mattress.

"You don't expect me to stay here," Kiesha said.

"Yes, and you will, " Samuel said.

"There's a TV to keep you occupied while we wait on the payment from Roman," he said as he shoved her onto the bed before he walked out of the room. For the first time she sobbed uncontrollably. Her stomach rumbled because she hadn't eaten breakfast and she had to use the bathroom. She got up from the bed and looked around the tiny room where there was a bucket in the corner that she assumed was used for waste.

"I am not using that," she said to no one in particular.

Just as she sat back on the bed Samuel entered the room with a tray of food, there were sandwiches and fruit and water. "Here you go," he said as he put the tray on the tiny table beside the bed. He walked over to Kiesha and caressed her smooth, brown skin, "you're beautiful like the women from my country."

Kiesha was light brown with short natural hair she looked like a younger version of Nia Long with a body like Teyana Taylor. Samuel continued to caress her face; he attempted to kiss Kiesha and she turned her face. He gripped her face and forced his tongue down her throat, Kiesha bit his tongue and he slapped her hard across the face.

"Bitch," Samuel said in a very thick accent. He ripped Kiesha's dress and exposed her breasts. He bit down on her breast, Kiesha screamed out in agony. Blood was dripping on her chest and her breast had begun to swell.

"Fucking bitch," he said again. He tried to turn Kiesha over on her stomach, but she struggled until she was exhausted. Samuel entered her anally and Kiesha pleaded for him to stop. He kept going. It didn't matter that it was hurting him more than it was hurting her. Please, please stop, she cried out. He temporarily stopped to lubricate his penis with the mayo from the sandwich he gave her to eat. Oh my God please don't do this she said as he massaged the condiment onto his shaft. Her pleads went unheard and he entered her again and this time he stroked her with vengeance.

"This will teach you to respect me," he said as he pounded away at her ass. You want a go boss Samuel said as Frantz walked in. "Oui" Frantz said. Samuel removed his member from Kiesha's ass, and she was grateful for this brief break. Frantz dropped his pants and revealed the biggest dick Kiesha had seen in her life. Frantz took a condom from his pants pocket and put it on his large shaft.

"Wash her off," Frantz said. "I like my pussy clean."

Samuel got dressed and left the tiny room he returned with warm towels and wet washcloth that smelled of lavender. Clean yourself Frantz said as he stroked his massive penis. Kiesha did as she was told because she did not want to enrage the men more. Frantz put his fingers inside of her pussy and smelled them to make sure she was cleaned properly.

"Unlike Samuel I like to treat my women tenderly," Frantz said, showing those hideous gold teeth. Frantz began kissing on Kiesha's neck, she laid back and let herself get lost in thought. Frantz entered her slowly because he knew his penis was large and Kiesha had the tightest pussy he had ever felt. She was dry and Frantz's dick was burning from the friction. He dripped a few drops of lube on his dick he had in his pants pocket and continued to enter her.

He was going at a slow rhythm and he noticed Kiesha's body was starting to respond. Kiesha was screaming inside because she had no control over her body. Kiesha was cursing herself inside and tears ran down her face. Frantz picked up the pace and was fucking Kiesha faster and she heard herself moan, tears fell even faster down her face because she didn't know why her body was betraying her. Frantz pumped at a fast-even stroke and before they both knew it Kiesha squirted everywhere. Frantz climaxed and left the room. Kiesha was left alone in the room with her thoughts.

Chapter 3

"I can't believe that happened," Kiesha said out loud. I did not want to enjoy sex with him. I was being forced against my will, but my body betrayed me. Kiesha sobbed all night until the next day. Samuel entered her room and she was afraid he would rape her again. This time he brought food along with a clean sweat suit. He gave her a water basin and washcloths so she could take care of her hygiene.

"Thank you," Kiesha said as he left the room. She ate her food in peace and laid down on the urine-stained mattress. She drifted off to sleep when Frantz came into the room and slapped her across the face. She woke up disoriented. He shoved a cellphone to her ear.

"Hello," she said lowly. "Kiesha is that you?" Roman asked.

"Romannnnnn" Kiesha screamed.

"I want my money in the next 48 hours, or your sweet little bitch is dead," Frantz said before he disconnected the phone.

Frantz snatched her off the bed and dragged her inside of the house.

"Please don't kill me" she begged.

"I'm not going to kill you yet. I am not going to keep going into that drab ass room to get some pussy, so you'll be in the guest room until payment is received."

'What," Kiesha said with a confused look on her face?

"Go, take a shower and I have something for you to wear lying on the bed."

"Nooooo," she said while clawing at Frantz's hand. He took his cigar from his mouth and burned her hand.

"Ughhhhhh," she screamed out.

"Ok, ok, ok I'll do it," she said. Kiesha stepped into the bedroom and noticed the black lace teddy laying on the bed. She cried while she got undressed. How did a rich girl become a drug dealers' pawn? She thought about Christmas at Chateau Elan, summers on Martha's Vineyard and she cried a little bit more.

"Hurry up in there." She heard Frantz say from the other side of the door. Kiesha took a quick shower and looked at the mirror her usually maintained hair had matted to her head, she had a bruise on her breast and now a burn mark on her inner thigh and hand. Her skin looked ashy and dry.

She moisturized her skin with the lotion that was in the bedroom. She combed her hair and added water to curl it. She was fixing herself up for Frantz but to remind herself of how gorgeous she was no matter what was going on.
"Beautiful" Frantz said as he entered the room and saw Kiesha dressed in the outfit he brought for her.
Frantz's dick became hardened by looking at Kiesha's sexy ass sitting on the bed.

"Stand up," he demanded. Kiesha did as she was told because the pain from the burn was lingering. Kiesha stood up and walked over to Frantz. He rubbed his hand over her supple ass. He has always admired Kiesha's beauty and wanted her to be with him. Frantz rubbed Kiesha's body and fondled her breast, she winced from the pain of Samuel biting her.

"Samuel's a fucking animal," Frantz said. "He doesn't know how to appreciate true beauty."

Frantz kissed Kiesha and she was nauseous to her stomach.

"Do a lil dance for me!" She turned her back to him and slowly danced, she turned her back to him because she didn't want him to see the tears that were forming in her eyes.

"Nice," he said and slapped her on the ass. "I've been wanting to fuck you for years. Roman doesn't know what to do with a woman like you." He was rubbing her ass and stroking his fat dick at the same time. He walked behind her, and she felt his large manhood against her backside. He tapped his dick on her behind and she panicked. His dick was entirely too big for him to do anal. She prayed that he wouldn't try it. Kiesha had to think fast. "Let me suck your dick," she said in a desperate tone. "No!," he replied loudly.

"Only whores do that and you're no whore," he said gruffly. He grabbed her hand and led her to the bed, she laid back nervously, her knees were shaking as well as her hands. "I'm not going to hurt you, this is business not personal," he informed her.

He pulled her panties to the side and entered her. After thirty minutes of constantly pounding her pussy Kiesha was sore and was hoping this would come to an end soon. She tried her hardest not to enjoy the sex, but it was damn near impossible, his dick touched places she didn't know existed. The more he pounded the creamier his dick became; she hated this shit. What the fuck are you thinking Kiesha, she said to herself? Finally, after an hour Frantz came and not only that but he did it inside of her without a rubber. Kiesha burst out crying, "why did you do that she screamed?"

Frantz slapped her. "Because I can," he said boldly.

"Who's here to stop me, Roman?" he said while laughing.

"Oh my God Roman please help me," she said loudly. Frantz laughed even louder. It seems he doesn't care for you because I would never let this happen to my woman.

"Come to the guess room."

"Yes boss," Samuel said as he opened the door.

"Samuel, I think she needs another lesson in respect."

"I'm sorry," she screamed as Samuel walked over to her.

"Shut up bitch, " he said as he punched her in the stomach as she laid on the bed. Kiesha coughed and cried loudly.

"I'm sorry," she pleaded as Samuel landed punches all over her body. She balled herself up to absorb some of the force and protect her body. She cried and begged but that only made it worse.

"That's enough Frantz barked don't fucking kill her you, idiot." Frantz forced Kiesha onto her stomach and entered her asshole, she passed out from the pain.

When Kiesha woke up she was back inside of the tiny dimmed lit room. Her whole body was sore, and she could barely move.

"Roman please!" she screamed. She scrambled around the room to find something to cover her body with, there was a t-shirt crumbled under the bed. It had a blood stain on it but at that moment Kiesha didn't care she just wanted to be home.

Chapter 4

"Roman are you going to answer your phone, " Bianca said as she was sucking Roman's dick?

"No, it's Kiesha and I don't want to be disturbed right now. Oh shit, suck it! Damn you good girl," he whispered.

"Bring that ass up here" Roman said. Bianca lifted her dress over her ass and slid down on Roman's waiting dick. Bianca bounced up and down on Roman's dick with each stroke she left trails of white cum down his dick.

"Oh fuck," he said.

"You like that, " Bianca said as she grinded harder on his dick. Roman stood up with Bianca on his lap.

He walked around the hotel room pounding away at her pussy. She screamed out in ecstasy and Roman came inside of her.

"I'm going to run a hot bath," Bianca said as she walked into the bathroom.

"Cool," Roman replied. Ring, ring, ring his cellphone interrupted him as he was preparing to get in the whirlpool.

"Hello," Roman said as he picked up the phone. There was silence on the other end then he heard Kiesha's voice, "Romannnnn!" she screamed through the phone.

"I want my money in 48 hours, or the bitch dies," he heard a voice say. "Frantz?" Roman asked.

"Yes, this is Frantz you assured me that I would not have any issues receiving payments but now you are late. Your lady is with me until I receive my payment in full plus 10% interest."

"Ahhhh!" Roman screamed as he tossed the phone across the room.

"What's going on?" Bianca inquired as she exited the bathroom.

"Get the fuck out," Roman barked. He poured a shot of Hennessy and tried to gather his thoughts. Roman quickly got dressed and went to his office, Case Co.

"Tiffany, can you call my accountant Mr. Waters and tell him I need him her in 20?"

"Yes, Sir," Tiffany replied.

He heard her making the call as he entered his office. He had several emails sent to him from an unknown sender. He clicked on the first email and a video instantly played. It was Samuel forcibly having anal sex with Kiesha. Roman touched the screen and tears fell down his face. Another video played and it was Frantz having sex with Kiesha and she squirted all over him. Roman became instantly upset. What the fuck he said and slammed the laptop closed. He poured himself another stiff drink and straightened his tie. His thoughts were interrupted when Tiffany announced Mr. Waters.

"Thanks, Tiffany can you please close the door behind you," said Roman.

"Roman, how are you?" John said as he extended his hand. "I'm not okay, I have a problem and I need your help. I need 2.5 million by tomorrow, I was approached about a new venture and time is of the essence," said Roman.

"This is me, Roman, what the fuck is going on?" said John. Roman stood up from his desk and checked the door to make sure no one was listening.

"It's Kiesha, Frantz has her and I need that money to get her back."

"Shit," John said under his breath.

"I'll do what I can, you know most of your money is tied up in this merger and it's too late to pull out now."

"I know," Roman said as tears fell down his face. "I love her man, I must get her back."

"I know," John said while patting Roman on the back.

"I don't know what I would do if something happened to her."

"I will get right on this Sir," John said.

"Thanks, so much," Roman said as he shook John's hand before he left the office. I need to tell Mr. Devereaux but I know he's never going to forgive me for letting anything happen to Kiesha. Fuck it here it goes!!

Roman pulled up to Devereaux Enterprises and let out a loud sigh. I might as well handle this like a man. Roman opened the door of his candy red 2019 Range Rover and headed towards the building. He was dressed in a black Tom Ford suit and black Alexander McQueen loafers.

His salt and pepper beard was neatly lined up and his hair was freshly cut. He looked like the real estate mogul he portrayed instead of the murderous drug dealer he was. He walked inside of the building and the secretaries looked up from their computer screens and flashed him a fuck me now smile. Roman kept walking because he had one thing in mind and that was to get his woman back. He walked past the secretary pool to Mr. Noah Devereaux's office.

"Roman Case for Mr. Devereaux," he said to the receptionist.

"Sure thing," she said as she buzzed his office.

"Roman, come in," said Mr. Devereaux.

"How have you been? It's been a long time since I've seen you, how have you been treating my princess?"

"That's the reason I am here sir, she has been kidnapped."

"What the fuck do you mean kidnapped?"

"Yes, Frantz took her and will not let her go until he receives 2.5 million dollars."

"Frantz, you mean to tell me you let that Haitian savage get his hands on my daughter. When I turned the business over to you, you assured me that you could handle it. You assured me that nothing would ever happen to my daughter." He slammed his hands on the desk.

"you ignorant, dumb, incompetent fool how could you be so damn reckless" Noah spewed.

"You stupid muthafucker do you know what would happen if my name is attached to some bullshit? I trusted you with my daughter and my business. Get the fuck out of my face before I kill you myself," Noah yelled looking at Roman in disgust.

Roman went to his car, shoulders slumped and a heavy feeling in his chest.

Chapter 5

I must get out of here Kiesha thought to herself or I am going to die. Another one of Frantz's goons came into the room and offered her food and water as well as a sweat suit and bandages for her wounds. He placed the items on the bed and left. She was relieved that this guy didn't try anything with her. Kiesha turned the TV on and saw a commercial for her father's real estate company. She immediately thought of home and she felt strength grow from deep down inside. She ate and used some of the water to clean her wounds and wrap them. She looked under the sweat suit and noticed a small surgical knife. She placed it under her mattress, she didn't know the new goon, but she was grateful for him.

Several hours passed and Kiesha was drifting off to sleep and suddenly Samuel entered the room and he had a black eye and he smelled of alcohol.

"Look what happened because of you, " he snarled. He went to grab Kiesha from the bed and she grabbed the knife and slit his throat.

Samuel's eyes grew large and he grabbed his throat. She pushed him to the floor. Blood was gushing everywhere, and a large pool was forming around his body. She reached in his pocket to get the key for the door. She looked up at the window in the room. She struggled to push it open after she unlocked it from the inside. She looked out the window as her eyes searched for any of Frantz's men outside. As she looked around and didn't see anyone so she climbed out the window. She jumped down and landed on her feet. Soon as she landed she took off running towards the dirt road. She didn't care that she was covered with blood and didn't have on any shoes. She ran and ran until she was out of breath, the air was thin, and it was beginning to snow.

She stopped for a moment until she was able to catch her breath. Just as she walked back on the dirt road, she saw a car coming towards her and she panicked because she thought it was one of Frantz's men to take her back. The car zoomed by her and then slammed on breaks; she took off running.

A familiar voice called out her name, it was her father. "Daddy, " Kiesha called out as she sprinted towards the car. Her father hugged her tightly.

"Daddy, how did you know to find me?"

"Roman came to me and told me what happened. He's a fucking idiot and I will never forgive him for putting you in harm's way."

"Daddy, I am fine."

"You're not fine to look at you, I'll have my doctor meet us at the compound," Noah said.

"Fine," she said because there was no need to argue with the great Noah Devereaux.

"How did you find me daddy?" she asked again.

"One of Frantz's guys was an old associate of mine, he called once he saw you in the house. Frantz will regret this," Noah stated angrily.

"I need to call Roman because I know he is worried sick," she said.

"Once we get to the jet you can call him and take a shower," her father said. Kiesha closed her eyes until they reached the small airport. She stepped aboard the Airbus A380 and was relieved to be away from all of the hurt and trauma dealing with Frantz.

She picked up the phone to call Roman, but he didn't pick up the phone, so she decided to take a shower and try later. She stepped inside of the shower and let the hot water wash away the stress of her traumatic experience. Her dad had her favorite body wash and shampoo stocked. He remembered Kiesha thought to herself and began to cry. She thought of the good times she had growing up as a child. It was nothing that she wanted or needed because she was Noah Devereaux's daughter and that meant she was basically royalty.

The Devereaux family had a multi-million-dollar real estate enterprise along with several small media companies. Kiesha was working as a real estate agent when she met Roman. She was intrigued by his tough guy exterior and after several months of dating she saw that it was more than what she saw on the surface.

Once Noah saw how Kiesha was serious about Roman and that he wasn't going away he took him under his wings and showed him the real estate business and turned over his drug empire to make sure his daughter never needed anything. Noah was very protective of Kiesha because she was his only child by his first wife who unfortunately passed away from breast cancer when Kiesha was only three years old. It was only her and her father for several years until he met his current wife Carmen. Kiesha hated Carmen and the feeling was mutual but Carmen wouldn't dare let Noah know it. Kiesha held Noah's heart and Carmen felt it every time she saw them together.

Kiesha called Roman again once she got out of the shower.

"Hello," Roman said as he picked up the phone.

"Hey, it's me," Kiesha said annoyed. "Kiesha, where are you?" he asked.

"I am on my father's jet headed to the compound."

"Are you ok?" he cried.

"I will meet you there?" She disconnected the call and rested until she reached her father's home. It had been years since she had been home mainly because of Carmen. The gated estate was in the heart of Buckhead, it sat on seventeen acres. The home resembled a Chateau located in the south of France. It had a carriage house as well as a pool house with a stocked lake. When Kiesha opened the door, Carmen was waiting near the winding staircase like a stepford wife. She walked past Carmen and headed to the master suite on the second floor which is where her childhood bedroom was located. Her little brother Francisco was in his room playing Call of Duty on his PS4.

"Take that bitch" he said into the microphone not noticing his sister was standing in the doorway.

She looked around his room and it looked like something out of a gamers dream. He was sitting on his black and red racing chair with a bottle of water sitting beside him. Red beanbag chairs were situated around the room, he had various Funko POP as well as video games on every shelf in his room. He had the latest Xidax PC and every pair of Jordan's imaginable.

"Hermano," Kiesha said to interrupt her brother out of his trance.

"Hermana," he said excitedly. He was happy to see his big sister.

"How have you been kiddo?" she asked while rubbing his curly hair. Kiesha was 15 years older than her brother but they always had a great relationship considering she was an only child for 15 years; she was excited to become a big sister.

"Where have you been?" Francisco asked. "Fuckkkkk," he said into the microphone mid-sentence while talking to his sister.

"Hey guys I'll be back," he said into the microphone before he muted it.

"I've been busy with work lately, but I promise I will start coming around more," she said as she kissed him on the forehead.

"I'm about to go up to my room. I just wanted to stop by first."

Kiesha stepped onto the elevator to go to her room. She stepped off the elevator and opened the white French doors to her bedroom suite. She could hear the water from the waterfall she had inside of her bathroom. She took her shoes off because she didn't want to get anything on her furry white carpet.

She ran her hand across her gold vanity set as she looked around her room. She sat on the stool and pulled out a Champion track-suit with white Filas. She wasn't in the mood to get dressed up. She combed her afro out and used a sponge to curl it up. She laid down on the bed to rest, she was physically and mentally exhausted. She was drifting off to sleep when she felt someone touch her leg. She woke up screaming and fighting but when she realized it was Roman, she calmed down.

"Roman," she cried as she hugged him.

"I am sorry baby, please forgive me," he said. "I can't believe I let this happen to you. Did they hurt you too bad?" he asked. "I will be okay," she said. "My father had his Doctor check me out. He also did an HIV and STD screening since they violated me." Kiesha burst into tears as she walked Roman through the whole incident until her escape.

Roman hugged her tightly and informed her Norman hired two men to the security team to make sure nothing like this ever happens again. "I can't have your father thinking I can't protect you," he said.

"He told me to take care of you and I am going to do just that."

Chapter 6

It was the perfect spring day in Atlanta Roman was riding down 285 in his Silver Audi R8. He weaved in and out of traffic headed to his warehouse in East Atlanta. He had the top down enjoying the breeze while the sounds of The Wu-Tang Clan C.R.E.A.M flowed through the speakers.

He nodded his head as he sang along to the classic. He felt unstoppable. His real estate business was booming, the woman he loved was home and his drug cartel was thriving. He pulled up to the warehouse and stepped out wearing an all-black Champion sweat suit with black Champion Timberlands. He was met by Blackboi, his trusted general within his organization. Blackboi was his childhood friend that he ran the streets with and who introduced him to the drug game, but it was Kiesha's father who taught him to treat it like a business.

"What up Killa," said Blackboi?

"It's all good baby," Roman said flashing his million-dollar smile. Blackboi was a dark skinned, dread head from Newark. He met Roman when he was a freshman in high school. One day Roman went to the bathroom and saw five guys attempting to jump Blackboi and he intervened, from that day forward they had been inseparable.

"Did you get the shipment in from Jersey?" Roman asked as he walked inside of the warehouse?

"Yes, everything is going according to schedule," Blackboi replied.

"I had to rundown on Lil Jay's ass he was cutting our shit and trying to skim money off top. I got the lil muthafucker in here."

Blackboi flipped the lights on and there was Lil Jay strung up with a chain and bleeding from his mouth and sides. He had passed out from the torture Blackboi and his boys put on him.

"Wake that muthafucker up," Roman said through clenched teeth. One of Blackboi's men slapped Lil Jay and he woke up screaming.

The group of men burst out laughing.

"Do you think you can steal from me?" Roman asked while pulling out his white and gold pistol from his waist.

"No," Lil Jay said as he begged for his life.

"I just needed more money, my girl is pregnant," he explained.

"And you couldn't come to me and ask me for more products?" Roman asked while shaking his head.

"I'm so sorry but I can't have anyone stealing from me. It's bad for business bruh," Roman said as he shot Lil Jay in the head. His body went instantly limp.

"You two muthafuckers get this body out of here," Roman said. "And this shit better not trace back to me or I'm killing you two also."

"Yes, boss," the men said in unison as they took the body down and went about the process of disposing of it.

"I need you to follow me to the spot," Roman said to Blackboi.

"For sure," he replied and got into his midnight blue 1968 charger and followed Roman to the West end.

The two got out of the car at the drab apartment complex walking towards Apt B and out of nowhere, they were bombarded with bullets. Roman ducked down behind his car and tried to see which direction the bullets were coming from. He heard someone call his name and continued to spray bullets from what seemed like an AK-47.

The bullets whizzed by swiftly and he heard Blackboi say, "Fuck this."

It was almost like a scene in a movie. Blackboi stood up from behind his car and unloaded his gun at the unknown shooter. He was hit in the neck and in the chest and his body fell lifeless beside Roman. The car finally sped off, it seemed like an eternity but only five minutes had passed. Roman crawled over to Blackboi and closed his eyes.

He cried like a baby because his best friend was dead, and it was nothing he could do about it. The tenants started to come out of their apartments and soon it was a huge crowd of onlookers crying and screaming. The ambulance and police sirens could be heard in the distance as much as he didn't want to, he had to leave his best friend laying alone on the hot pavement because he could not chance being caught in the area.

Roman hopped into his car and fled the scene. He did not want to leave his best friend, but he didn't have a choice. He kept replaying the events in his mind. He was certain the shooter had a Haitian accent. In all the years he had been in the drug game he never had anyone to run down on him. Roman was seeing red and wanted blood from whoever was responsible.

Did they know he was the great Roman Case and Noah Devereaux was his future father in law? No one in the state of Georgia would rest until this was dealt with. He called Noah to let him know what had transpired. He dialed Noah's cell number and it went straight to voicemail. He decided to go to his condo in Midtown.

When he walked through the door the smell of patchouli and sandalwood filled the air. Kiesha was sitting on the floor with her eyes closed and various stones around her. He assumed she was meditating and didn't want to disturb her, but she opened her eyes when she felt him standing near her.

"What's up babe?" She said as she opened her eyes and noticed blood was all over his clothes and face.

"Oh my god! What happened baby" she said panicking.

"Are you hurt?"

"I am fine but Rashad isn't," he said.

"Some shooters came after us when we went to the spot today and I swear one of them had a Haitian accent."

"Do you think it could be retaliation for Frantz?" she asked.

"I don't know baby, but I can't let a muthafucker get away with that shit," he said forcefully.

"I'm about to take a shower," he said through tears.

"Ok baby," she said as she gathered her stones and blew out her candles.

Roman went to the bedroom and when Kiesha heard the shower starting she decided to call her father. She dialed her father's cell and there was no answer. She put her cell phone away and joined Roman. She pulled her t-shirt over her head and slipped out of her underwear. She stepped inside of the shower and hugged Roman from the back, he jumped because he didn't hear her come in due to the music playing and the rainfall shower head. She kissed him on his neck, and he turned around and held her tightly. His tears blended in with the water from the shower.

She could see the hurt and anguish on his face. She held him tightly as well and kissed him deeply. He picked her up and slid his pulsating dick inside of her. She was nervous because they hadn't made love since she had been kidnapped and was still healing emotionally and physically but he felt amazing. When he slid inside of her, she screamed out in ecstasy. He never heard or felt Kiesha's body react this way. He was mesmerized by her moans and screams, he almost forgot that it was the worst day of his life.

Flashes of his friend killed flooded his mind and he fucked her harder. She cried out in pain and pleasure. Roman released and started to cry uncontrollably.

Kiesha was taken aback by his reaction; in all the years of them being together she never saw him vulnerable. She held him tightly and he cried even more.

"I am so sorry baby, " he said through tears. "It seems everything I love, I seem to lose or hurt. Can you please forgive me?" he said.

"I forgive you baby. I knew what I signed up for when I entered this relationship. I know you love me, but I also know the kind of man you are. It's ok," she reassured him.

"I really need to get in touch with your father," he said.

"I tried to call him earlier, but he didn't answer," Kiesha replied.

After Roman stepped out of the shower he got dressed and hopped into his black 1996 Camry. Kiesha knew whenever he got into that car, he wanted to be incognito and someone was destined to die. She said a quick prayer to the ancestors to cover him through this trying time. She didn't want to stay in the house alone, so she called her girl, KK.

"Hey girl," KK said as she answered on the first ring.

"Damn girl you must've been sitting by the phone," Kiesha laughed.

"I need to get out for a little while."

The two met when KK worked for her father. KK was Afro-Asian and didn't mind telling what was exactly on her mind. KK was a natural beauty, her long curly black hair, full lips, brown skin, and slanted eyes made her look like a goddess. KK left her father's company five years ago and since had become a social media influencer.

Chapter 7

Kiesha hopped into her car and headed for KK's house. Once she arrived KK greeted her with a glass of cranberry prosecco, Kiesha's favorite. Even though KK was an influencer her home was bigger than most entertainers.

"Kiesha, I knew you didn't want to be home alone, and I didn't feel like going to the clubs. I hired a chef and a bartender to make sure we enjoy our night," said KK.

"The chef prepared a seafood tower along with a crudité and charcuterie platter." Kiesha was impressed with how KK was able to set that up in such a short period.

"Everything looks amazing and I am ready to enjoy my night," Kiesha said as she held her glass up to KK's. "Cheers!" They both said as the glasses hit each other.

"Girl, I am so glad you called me because I was wanting to host a social media event and wanted to know what would your dad think about me hosting it at his mansion?" KK said.

"I have no clue, but I am sure he will let you use it," Kiesha said as she let out a little giggle.

"Tell me what's been going on in your world?"Kiesha asked. " It's been so long since I heard from you KK."

"Well, as you know I am popping on Instagram now," KK said as she fanned herself showing her bottom grill.

"I am planning this social media event to bring awareness to the BLM movement and raise money."

"That sounds amazing, girl and I will be happy to assist in any way I can," Kiesha uttered.

"Thanks so much and you know I am going to need your help," KK said while the bartender filled both lady's glasses.

"I am so grateful for this down time; it has been so hectic lately. Honestly thank you KK," Kiesha replied with tears in her eyes.

"You're welcome and I am happy to be here for you."

"What's going on with you girl? You haven't been yourself in a while," KK replied.

"You know how stuff is with Roman and on top of that Blackboi got killed so now it's going to be more drama and chaos. I am just tired of all the baggage that comes with his lifestyle. I've been kidnapped, raped, and tortured. How much more am I supposed to sacrifice being with him? I was fucking debutante for Christ sakes," Kiesha said laughing with tears falling from her eyes.

"I am serious. KK. I've had proposals from freaking princes and shit. Instead I am here taking shit from Roman. I'm exhausted from this and I don't know how much more I can stand," she stated matter of factly.

"I feel you girl these street niggas are exhausting. That's why I prefer a certain standard of man, you know like Noah Devereaux," KK burst out laughing. "I'm only joking but I'm serious, girl."

"I know KK but I love him, and we have been through so much together. I feel like I owe it to us to see it through."

"Ok girl," KK said while firing up a blunt. "Here," KK said, passing the blunt to Kiesha.

"I need this muthafucker," she said while laughing.

"Tell me more about this event you're trying to plan? I think this is such a great idea," Kiesha said while exhaling the smoke.

"You know all this crazy shit that has been going on since the guy that got killed in Minnesota and I want to do something positive," said KK.

"I was thinking of inviting The Who's who of Atlanta, athletes, and entertainers. I want it to be the black-tie event of the season. I want The Great Gatsby theme; you know, elegant."

"That sounds amazing and I am sure my dad will let you use the estate. I will reach out to him tomorrow for you,"Kiesha replied.

&&&

Roman was filled with rage as he drove back to the apartments where he and Blackboi were ambushed. Tears stung his eyes as he reminisced about all the times they shared growing up. He decided to give Noah a call to let him know what was going on, but his phone went straight to voicemail.

"Damn it, why this nigga doesn't never answer his phone," Roman screamed.

When he pulled up to the dilapidated building there were red and blue lights flashing all over the place. Yellow tape was around the building and a larger crowd had formed than earlier. He let the window down to see if he could hear anything about who could have done this. The neighborhood was no stranger to violence but seeing Blackboi outlined in chalk did something to the hood and you could feel the grief in the air.

Roman watched the crowd to see if anyone stood out. He noticed two guys he's never seen before whispering and pointing towards Blackboi's body. He continued to watch the gentlemen because something stood out about those two. He noticed the body language of the men. He was deep into thought when it was interrupted by the buzz of his cellphone.

It was Kiesha, he didn't want to answer but it could be an emergency he thought to himself. Buzz buzz the phone continued to vibrate but just as he was about to answer he noticed another man walked up to the other men and it hit him, it was the triggerman.

Roman pulled his gun from underneath the car seat and was about to get out of the car but he decided to follow them whenever they left the scene. The men smirked and walked away at the same time. The three piled into one small car. Roman watched as they left and followed them as they exited the apartment complex.

He stayed two cars behind to make sure he wasn't noticed. He followed them two hours out of the city to Wilkes County. Where the fuck are they going Roman thought to himself?

He followed them until they turned onto a dirt road. He parked his car and grabbed his .22 from under the seat. He pulled his hood down and headed down the dusty road. He spotted a raggedy barn and hid in the bushes to see if he could figure out what was going on.

He spotted the three men through a broken window. He listened to see if he could hear what was being said but they were speaking in French. Why couldn't these motherfuckers be speaking Spanish Roman chuckled to himself. His thoughts were disturbed when he heard one of them say his name. He knew it had to be something connected to Blackboi. He pulled his phone out to use the translator when his phone buzzed again. "Fuck," Roman said out loud. He was holding his breath hoping the three strangers didn't hear his phone, but it was too late. They gathered their guns from the table and headed outside to see where the noise was coming from. Roman bent down lower to stop from being noticed but it didn't work.

"Roman Case," the stranger mumbled while he held a gun to the back of Roman's head.

"Get up nigga, " he said as he pushed the gun into Roman's back.

"Jay, Lee come here and look and see what I have." The guys trotted over and started laughing when they noticed Junior had Roman.

"Looka hea," Lee said as he punched Roman in the stomach. Lee was the enforcer of the trio. He was 6'6'' with muscles. His locs hung on his back and he had a God's son tattoo across his stomach. Roman winced in pain and coughed to try and catch his breath.

"Good job Junior at least your fat ass is good for something,"
Jay said. He patted Junior on the back and caressed his scruffy beard.
Roman spit on the ground as a sign of disrespect to the three men.

Lee punched him again but this time in the face. Roman could
tell instantly his nose was broken. He thought to himself that he needs
to get out of this situation, but he didn't have a clue as to how he was
going to do it. Junior's belly jiggled as he laughed. Junior was the
pudgy one out of the trio.

Roman was trying to see if it was physically possible to fight
the trio, he knew he could take Jay and Junior but Lee was a different
story. The guys began to speak in French as they led Roman inside of
the barn. Roman's phone began to buzz, Lee snatched the phone and
threw it in the bushes. The barn was filled with barrels of cocaine and
rows and rows of marijuana on storage shelves. The air was filled
with musk and marijuana. The barn looked raggedy outside, but the
inside was an impressive warehouse. Roman had to hand it to them.
No one would ever think to look for millions of dollars' worth of
drugs in a small country town in a raggedy barn. Well played he
thought to himself. The guys tied Roman to a pipe inside of the
building and stepped outside to make a phone call.

"Junior stay back and watch him," Lee barked to him.

"I'm sick of him," Junior said as he walked towards Roman.

"Why did you follow us?" Junior asked Roman.

"We saw you in the parking lot watching us. I never wanted to
kill Blackboi," Junior confessed.

Roman's blood began to boil.

"You motherfucker," Roman said as he kicked at Junior.

"You better be glad I'm tied up because I will kill you."

"I'm sorry man," Junior said as he lowered his head. Lee and
Jay bombarded the door with guns drawn.

3 "What the fuck is going on in here?" Jay asked, looking puzzled. "Nothing Jay," Junior said.

"I got it man, I'm sick of you checking up on me like I am a fucking baby. You worked for my dad, don't forget that shit," Junior huffed.

Jay spun around and headed back outside. Lee shook his head and followed Jay outside.

"I am so sick of those two," Junior said as he lit his spliff and inhaled.

"Why do you deal with those ordering you around?" Roman inquired.

"I guess because we grew up together in Haiti and my dad wanted me to keep them around since their fathers worked for him. Fucking Frantz man," Junior exclaimed.

Frantz, Roman thought to himself. He started breathing rapidly as he envisioned the bullet Kiesha put in the back of Frantz's head. Just as Roman was about to question Junior the other two men walked in.

Chapter 8

Noah Devereaux's mansion was dripped with black and gold, the who's who of Atlanta came out to the black lives matter gala that KK was hosting. Noah walked down the stairs and the room grew quiet as he walked into the room.

He was dressed in a black tuxedo with a gold bow tie. His regal demeanor gave him a look of royalty, the ladies began to blush as he walked through the room. KK was standing by the champagne fountain when she spotted Noah.

"I've been looking for you all afternoon," she said as she touched his muscular chest.

"Well here I am, young lady," he said as he touched her hand.

"This turn out is great," he said.

"I'm so excited to do something for the community. I never thought that I could make a difference."

Just as the two were talking Kiesha walked up.

"Hey dad, " she said as she hugs Noah tightly.

"This is wonderful KK, and did you see Angela Terrell and Domaneque Credle, they are the owners of rekindled desires?"

"No, I didn't," Noah said. "But I will catch up with him later."

"Where is Roman?" KK asked.

"I have no clue I've been looking for him all day. He was supposed to be here tonight, but I haven't heard from him all day. I tracked his phone, but it seems he is in Wilkes County. I don't know why the fuck he is even there. Dad, have you heard from Roman today?"

"No, I haven't," Noah said. "But it is imperative that I speak with him immediately." KK walked off to greet more guests.

"It seems he has been messing up lately. When I turned my business over to him, he assured me that he could handle it. I'm trying to run for governor In a few years and I don't need this type of issue."

"I know that dad," Kiesha said as she grew irritated.

"I gave him not only my empire, but I trusted him with you. Then he lets you get kidnapped and not only that you must deal with all those other women. Don't think I don't know what's going on. I have people everywhere and they tell me things. When I first met him, you told me you guys were getting serious and he assured me that he would treat you like the Princess you are."

"He's trying dad," Kiesha said.

"Trying isn't enough," Noah said.

"I need him to follow through on his promises." Kiesha was upset by the conversation, so she decided to excuse herself. Kiesha went to the bar to get a gin and tonic.

KK noticed Noah was now by himself and his wife Carmen was nowhere in sight. She gave him the signal they used when she worked for him years ago. KK was waiting inside of the wine cellar butt naked and heels on. Noah unbuttoned his tuxedo jacket and loosened his tie as he walked over to KK. Noah was fifty but very fit for his age. He had broad shoulders and a six pack thanks to his personal trainer. His salt and pepper beard and bald head made him irresistible. His chiseled body and tattooed skin made him look like an athlete.

"It's been a long time Mr. Devereaux," KK said as she unbuttoned his pants, his manhood sprung forth and KK was impressed.

It had been years since the two were together, but he was just as impressive as he was five years ago. She removed his shirt and began kissing all over him. Even though Noah was married KK was in love with him. She missed his strong hands caressing her back side. His deep voice and commanding presence. KK knew it was wrong to sleep with her friends' father, but she couldn't resist the great Noah Devereaux.

Noah ran his fingers through KK's hair slightly grabbing a chunk of her hair. He yanked her head back and kissed her neck. She let out a loud moan. Her womanhood dripped and throbbed. She hopped on the island inside of the cellar. Noah kissed the inside of her legs and pressed his hands against her love button. She gyrated and cried out from the electricity shooting through her body. Noah kissed her clit and began to eat her like he never had before. She was shaking from the waves of orgasms she experienced. He knew she was satisfied but he had more to give her. He lifted her off the island and placed his dick inside of her. He pumped vigorously until she creamed all over him. Noah knew it was time to explode, he choked KK as he ejaculated.

They were both spent but needed to get back to the party. KK cleaned up in the bathroom adjacent to the wine cellar and went back to the party. She left first and was just in time for the keynote speaker, Fred Quinn to give his speech. He was an aspiring politician and prominent businessman in the Atlanta area. The speaker had everyone in tears as he spoke about his humble beginnings and how he overcame injustice in life.

KK approached the podium and thanked everyone for coming out, the crowd was clearing out and Kiesha decided to call Roman again, but he didn't answer.

"Where are you, " Kiesha said out loud.

"What's going on pumpkin?" Noah asked.

"Nothing, Roman isn't answering my calls and I've been calling him the majority of the evening."

"I'm sure he's fine," he said. "Probably with some whore."

"Dad!" Kiesha exclaimed. Carmen, Noah's wife made her way over to speak since she had avoided Kiesha all night.

"Hi Kiesha," she said with her thick Spanish accent.

"Hi Carmen," Kiesha said dryly. It was obvious that the two women did not like each other. Noah interrupted the tension between the women.

"Carmen, where have you been this evening, you look absolutely stunning," he said as he kissed her forehead.

"I was making sure no one was stealing any of our things," she replied.

"Our things," Kiesha guffawed. "You mean my father's things because if memory serves me correctly you've never had a job."

Noah cleared his throat. "Pumpkin, let's not do this here."

"Sorry dad," Kiesha said. Kiesha called KK over knowing that it would make her stepmother uncomfortable. KK sashayed over, she looked like a model in her black mermaid-style gown. It hugged her curves perfectly; her long black, silky hair touched her back. Her makeup was flawless, she was gorgeous, and she knew it.

"Hello Mrs. Devereaux," KK said with a smirk on her face.

"Congratulations on your event, it was amazing," Carmen replied while looking at KK suspiciously.

"Thank you, ma'am, " she said, turning her attention to Kiesha.

"Yes, Kiesha," KK said.

"What are you doing after this," Kiesha asked?

"I am going to make sure the movers put everything back in place and Mr. Devereaux's home is spotless and everything is accounted for, then I am going home. This has been a draining day and I need rest."

Kiesha decided to head home and wait for Roman. Once inside of her vehicle she called him again and he still didn't answer. She tracked his phone and it was still in the same place. This man really thinks hecan keep fucking over me and I won't do anything she thought to herself. She pulled into the garage of their condo and tried his number once again. She went upstairs to undress and took a bubble bath.

She stepped into the tub and soaked until she fell asleep. When she awakened, she realized Roman was still not home nor returned her calls. She decided to get dressed and locate him. Something told her that something more serious was going on. She put on her black timberlands, black Nike tights and hoodie.

She opened the door to her closet and walked in to locate her guns inside of her antique trunk. She grabbed the sawed off shotgun, .40 caliber, and she put a 22 in the holster on her leg. She checked the location once again before she headed out the door. Kiesha hopped into her father's old school caddy a candy coated 1978 Cadillac Brougham with gold Dayton's, she placed the guns in a secret compartment of the trunk and set the GPS. Kiesha loved long drives by herself because it gave her time to reflect on her life. She really hated Roman at times because of the inconsiderate things he did. But she loved him more than any man she has ever been with.

She had a bad feeling that something else was going on, Roman had never gone this many hours without speaking to her. She tracked the phone once again and it was still at the same location, Kiesha turned the music up and drove the next hour to the small town.

What the hell Kiesha thought as the scenery changed from city to country. The pastures and overgrowth of bush were something Kiesha was not used to seeing.

"What in the world is Roman doing down here," Kiesha said out loud. She lit the blunt she had in the ashtray to calm her nerves as she grew closer to the location, Kiesha knew something was wrong and she couldn't shake it. She turned on the dirt road and noticed Roman's car was parked on the side of the road. She turned off her lights and the engine to the car. She got out and examined to see if she could see Roman or any signs of foul play.

There was nothing out of the ordinary with his car. She went to the trunk to retrieve her weapons. She put the bag over her shoulder and cocked her Glock before she headed down the dark road. Kiesha was paranoid from all the noises that were coming from the dark. She was not used to the stillness of the night. Kiesha continued to track Roman's phone until she heard men talking in the distance.

Chapter 9

Jay, Lee, and Junior were sitting around in the warehouse discussing what to do with Roman when they heard a noise coming from outside. Junior went outside to check it out, but he didn't see anything, but he kept hearing a buzzing noise. He walked around the perimeter but didn't see anything, but the noise was driving him insane. He walked a little farther and noticed a cellphone, damn he thought to himself, before he could tell the other guys he saw a flash of light and his body hit the ground. Kiesha picked up the phone and noticed it was Roman's. She turned it off and put it in her bag. She tiptoed closer and discovered a warehouse.

"I wonder what is taking Junior's fat ass so long," Lee huffed.

"He messed up everything we fucking do, if it wasn't for his dad, we wouldn't have to deal with shit."

He paced back and forth inside of the warehouse.

"I'm about to pop this nigga," Lee said to Jay.

"We have been waiting for hours on what to do with this motherfucker and I am sick of waiting. My bitch at home waiting on me," Jay chimed in with equal disgust of the situation.

"What do y'all want with me?" Roman asked.

"I've got money; I'll pay you triple of whatever you stand to make for killing me?

"I heard you say you're sick of baby-sitting fat boy. I can make you both lieutenants in my organization. Whatever you want is at your disposal."

Lee and Jay walked away and started speaking in French. Roman cracked a smile because he knew money was always a great decision maker. The men continued talking and Lee started getting louder, and Jay stormed off to the small office in the back of the building. Lee walked over to Roman and smacked him across the face with a closed fist. Roman's tooth became loose and he spit out blood.

"Fuck you," Lee screamed. "Do you think we are stupid? No amount of money will take the place of the satisfaction I will get from killing you." Lee spit at Roman's feet and joined Jay in the office.

"Did you really think about taking his money?" Jay asked.

"Yes," Lee replied.

"I'm sick of working for Frantz, dead or not, they think they own us. I'm no one's slave. I'm my own man. We've been putting in work since we were tikes and we're not one step closer to paying our family's debt. We're trapped," Lee said as he hit the desk.

"Killing him will pay off that debt. Boss man said it himself, Jay said.

"Boss man is dead or did you forget, that's why we're training Junior to take over. We should be taking over not him. I say we kill that fat man and blame it on Roman," said Lee.

&&&

Devereaux Estate

"Noah, I know it's no need to argue about it, but I do not like the way your daughter treats me in my own home," said Carmen.

"Carmen, I am not about to get into this same discussion with you again about my daughter, " he said, raising his voice.

"You are so jealous and it's unattractive. You live in this beautiful estate, you have a personal stylist, chef, trainer, and chauffeur what could you possibly have to be jealous about?"

Carmen screamed, "your heart; I don't have your heart."

"What are you talking about," Noah hollered back.

"I give you everything, you even have my son and you're jealous because of the relationship I have with my daughter, are you fucking kidding me? My daughter, who lost her mom when little girls need them the most, you really have a nerve. I cannot do this tonight because we have workers cleaning up and KK is still here overseeing everything."

"KK," Carmen said and gave him a death glare.

"Yes, KK, is there a problem with that dear?" he asked.

"Yes, it's a problem, everyone can come through my home and have all access to my husband."

Noah lit a cigar and blew the smoke in Carmen's face and walked away.

"Fuck you," Carmen said as she stormed to the elevator to go upstairs. She knew it was a lot to be married to Noah and she figured she could handle it. He was just a wallet to her when they first met but throughout the years she has grown to love and admire him. She tried to have a relationship with Kiesha, but she shut her out a long time ago and there was no future for their relationship.

As she entered the bedroom suite she took off her heels and dropped her ball gown in the middle of the floor. The tears began to fall as she ran her fingers along with her custom-made dresser. Carmen grew up poor in El Salvador and the lifestyle was sort of a fairy tale for her. She had a rich and powerful man, a gorgeous mansion, and a handsome son. It was enough for a while but as the years passed she wanted more of a connection with her husband. More tears fell as she thought of her son and how he doesn't completely have his father's heart. She wiped her tears and ran a bath to soak her worries away.

"There you are," Noah said as he snuck up behind KK and kissed her on the neck.

"I'm sorry may I help you, Mr. Devereaux," KK said as she cut her eyes towards the men cleaning up.

"It's fine," he said.

"I made all the help sign a nondisclosure agreement."

"Can you guys excuse us for a minute," KK said to the workers.

" Noah, you know we agreed to never show affection in public."

"This isn't, public, this is my home," he said boastfully.

"I can't help myself you look so beautiful tonight; I can't take my hands or eyes off you."

Noah caressed her shoulders and ran his fingers under her dress. He pressed against her love button and she let out a sigh.

"How does that feel, " he said gruffly. All KK could do was moan.

"Look at me," he commanded, she whimpered and began to stare deeply into his eyes. He moved his fingers more vigorously and soon KK was standing in a puddle of her juices.

"Wow," Noah said as he felt her squirting down his hand. He was dripping by that moment and had to have her. He picked her up and pounded her against the wall. He pounded until he became weak at the knees. After he exploded KK fixed her dress and found the workers to complete the cleanup. Noah took the elevator to the bedroom suite. He stepped off and saw Carmen's dress and heels in the middle of the floor. He followed suit and walked into the bathroom naked. Carmen was in the bath with her eyes closed enjoying the serene atmosphere.

Noah gently grabbed her by the throat, she opened her eyes to see Noah standing over her and his manhood staring her in the face. Her nipples aroused and electricity flowed through her lower region. She placed her mouth on Noah's member and took him whole. She was great at pleasing a man, it was a quality that he loved about her.

Carmen worked faster and faster to get Noah to cum. He moaned and groaned until he exploded in her mouth. She swallowed and he kissed her deeply. Carmen stepped out of the tub dripping wet, her perky breast and round ass, dark colored skin turned Noah on even more and he instantly became hard again. Her perfect physique and grace when she walked were like a sleek cat. She laid back on the bed and Noah dived in face first, he licked and nibbled, she screamed out in ecstasy. He knew she was ripe for the picking. He slid into her and they both moaned loudly. He lifted her legs over his shoulder and stroked long and hard. She screamed and screamed like she was being murdered but the only thing dying was her pussy.

"Let me get on top," she said between breaths. She rode him like a stallion until he bussed again, they held each other and went to sleep.

Chapter 10

Kiesha listened as she heard the strangers plan on killing someone named Junior. She was spooked when someone said the name Frantz, she began to sweat and tremble.

"Get it together," Kiesha said as she shook the nervousness off. She moved closer to the building to see if she could see Roman. Roman had his eyes closed and didn't notice Kiesha looking inside of the building. Lee and Jay burst outside of the office, Kiesha bent down and headed to the back of the building.

"How much are you trying to pay again?" Jay asked Roman.

"I'll triple whatever you stand to make from killing me," Roman stated.

"150 K," Lee said. "You'll really pay us that," he said with excitement.

"Yes, I'll gladly pay you a half a mil," Roman said boastfully.

"We just need you to do something for us as a gesture of good faith," said Lee. "What is it?" Roman asked.

"We need you to kill the fat boy for us."

"Why would I want to do that? It serves me no purpose killing him," said Roman.

"Either you want this money or not, " Roman said.

"We want it but how do we know you won't cheat us," said Lee.

"I am a man of my word and I always pay my debts. I just need to make a call to my girl to bring the money to you. It'll take her a few hours to get here but she will come," said Roman.

"I need to use one of you guys' phones to call her."

"Here, you can use mine," said Jay.

Roman dialed Kiesha's number but it rang with no answer.

Kiesha looked down at her phone and saw an unknown number calling, she sent the phone straight to voicemail.

"She didn't answer," Roman said.

"I will try again later but tell me more about why I should kill that young man for you."

"We are in debt to Frantz and we must not only work off this debt but show his son the ropes," said Lee.

"But Frantz is dead, so why do you have to pay off a debt to a dead man," said Roman.

"In this business we take on our parents' debt, it's been five years and we haven't gotten one step closer to being free of this nightmare," said Lee.

"Let's say I kill the other guy how do I know you won't try to pin it on me because you're scared of what's going to happen to you."

"I give you my word, we just want freedom and protection," said Jay.

"I'll do it, " said Roman. "But the main question is how are we going to do it? We need a plan and it must be flawless."

Roman had no intentions of killing just Junior, he wanted to kill them all for what they did to Blackboi. He was not a very forgiving person and since the moment his friend's body hit the pavement, he knew someone was going to pay. He asked to use the phone again to call Kiesha. Kiesha looked down at her phone and saw the unknown number flash across the screen, she pressed ignore once again.

Damn it, why the fuck isn't she answering the phone Roman said to himself.

"Ok guys I don't know why my lady isn't answering but I promise that I will have your money."

"We believe you," Lee said as he handed Roman the gun and called for Junior to come inside. Kiesha was down when she heard a voice calling out for Junior. Her pulse raced and she gripped the gun tighter as she prepared for whatever may come her way. Lee walked outside to look for Junior.

"Where the fuck are you Junior," he said as he walked through the brushes. He noticed Junior's limp body and as he turned to run towards the warehouse Kiesha shot him in the back of the head. She stood over his body and removed the gun from his waist. Kiesha walked closer and noticed Roman standing in the middle of the floor; clothes bloody, phone in hand and a gun in the other.

Kiesha looked down at her phone and decided to call the unknown number back, when she did Roman picked up on the first ring. "Duck" was all she said when the phone connected. Roman hung up the phone and bent down like he was about to tie his shoe.

"What the fuck is going on?" Jay said when Roman bent down. "What's going on?" Roman asked angrily.

He walked towards the front door and Kiesha burst inside the warehouse door and shot Jay in the chest. He was stunned momentarily but it didn't stop him from charging at Kiesha. He knocked her to the ground and knocked the gun from her hand. They struggled over the gun until Roman limped over to where they were at. He hit Jay over the head with the gun he had in his hand.

Kiesha slowly got up from the ground. She was bruised but it was bearable.

"How in the hell did you know I was here," said Roman.

"I tracked your phone and I saw your car and I decided to walk to see if I could see where you were. That's when I found this warehouse. I saw you and I waited until I saw someone walk outside. Then I shot him," she said.

"Do you know who that was?" Roman asked.

"No, I don't," she replied.

"It was Frantz Jr," Roman shouted.

"You must be fucking kidding me," Kiesha said as she let out a labored breath.

"I think this motherfucker cracked my rib," Kiesha said as she walked over to Jay's unconscious body and put a bullet in his head.

"Damn baby did you body all these mother fuckers?" Roman asked.

"You know who my fucking dad is, don't play," she laughed.

"Well damn let me call the guys down here to clean these bodies up," Roman said.

"Will you look at all this product in here," Kiesha said as she walked around and saw shelves full of drugs.

"I'm already on it Roman said," as he got the clean up crew on the phone. Kiesha and Roman bumped fist and they began to break down the bodies until the crew arrived. They struggled to get Junior's body inside of the warehouse.

"I have the bag outside with some of the tools we need to do this." Roman watched Kiesha as she punctured the guy's lung and chopped limbs. She was surgical with a knife and deadly with a gun. Roman hadn't seen that side of Kiesha before and it turned him on.

"How did you learn to do all this?" Roman asked.

"Jimmy, he used to work for my dad until the day he died. My dad never wanted me to know this side of the business, but Jimmy knew that I should be prepared in case I ever needed this set of skills. I would watch for hours as Jimmy broke down a body and do the real stuff that no one ever wanted to do. Yes, Jimmy taught me that, but dad was the one who taught me how to shoot." Kiesha's face lit up as she reminisced on Jimmy and her dad.

"I must say I am impressed with you Ms. Devereaux."

"Well thank you Mr. Case." Roman leaned over to peck Kiesha on the lips. Kiesha was finishing up when her phone rang, it was Russell, the cleaner.

"Are you guys here," Roman said.

"Come on down the road about a mile and you will see the warehouse."

Russell stepped out of the truck and he looked menacing. "Who did this," Russell said as he looked over at the bodies, he put his hand on his chin and stared at them.

" I did," Kiesha said. "What's wrong?"

"Nothing, it reminds me of my dad."

"Was your dad's name Jimmy?" Kiesha asked.

"How do you know him," Russell asked.

"He worked for my dad, but he was sort of a mentor for me growing up. I'm Kiesha nice to meet you," she said as she extended her hand.

"Kiesha?" he asked. "Noah Devereaux's daughter?" he asked.

"That's me," she said.

"My dad talked about you all the time, he loved you like the daughter he never had."

"Aww thanks," she said as a tear fell.

"You did a great job but it's time for me to do mine." Russell started the cleanup and two other men helped. Roman started loading the back of the truck with the product and when everything was cleaned Roman, Kiesha, and Russell left never to return to the scene.

Kiesha and Roman walked to their cars in silence. "I appreciate you coming to my rescue, I know that I haven't been the man you needed me through the years. I have disrespected you and your father with my selfish ways. I didn't appreciate you as the asset you are in my life," said Roman.

"I appreciate your candor," Kiesha said.

"I let you lead not because I am not capable, but I know the man you can become if you get out of your way. My father left his business to you, not because of our relationship but he saw a lot of himself inside of you. He wanted to help you grow to your full potential."

"I understand that now," Roman replied. They hugged and got into their separate cars and headed to the city. Once they arrived in the city Kiesha and Roman met up to get rid of the guns and bloody clothes. They had done this a few times before, but it was something special about this time. Roman looked at Kiesha and walked over to her.

"Kiesha I know this is crazy to even do this here, but will you marry me?" Kiesha looked over to Roman.

"Yes, I will marry you," she said.

"I've been waiting on this day for a while now," she said as she chuckled.

"Let's get out of here before someone sees us," Kiesha said.

Later that evening Kiesha and Roman decided to break the news to her father, Noah.

"Dad, we have something to tell you," Kiesha said.

"What is it," Noah said as he looked directly at Roman.

"Mr. Devereaux you know Kiesha and I have been together for a couple of years and I really love her with everything inside of me; even though I haven't been the best boyfriend, my love for her didn't change. I asked her to marry me and she agreed."

"Is this true?" Noah asked.

"Yes, it's true he asked me to marry him and I said I would. This isn't going to be a quick engagement because he has a few more things to show me before I walk down the aisle with him."

"Congratulations," he said to Kiesha.

"Welcome to the family Roman. Do right by my daughter or I will kill you myself," Noah said as he patted Roman on the back. Noah chuckled but he was serious, he would kill anyone who hurt his daughter.

Noah called to Charles, his longtime butler, and friend.

"Mr. Charles could you please retrieve some champagne from the wine cellar for us, it seems my daughter is about to get married."

"Congratulations, Ms. Kiesha," Charles said and disappeared downstairs.

Carmen came down the stairs dressed in a white halter top dress that hugged her curves, she had gold jewelry and sandals to match. She looked like a model from a magazine. Kiesha hated Carmen but she had to admit her dad had great taste in women. Noah walked over to greet Carmen with a kiss when she reached the bottom of the staircase.

"Honey Mr. Charles is going to get champagne because it's a celebration,"Noah said.

"What are we celebrating?" she asked.

"I asked Kiesha to marry me, Mrs. Devereaux," Roman said.

"That's wonderful," she said as she cracked a small smile.

"Kiesha may I speak with you in the day room," she said as she cleared her voice.

"Sure," Kiesha said uncertainly, as to what Carmen may have wanted to talk to her about.

Kiesha followed Carmen from the great room to the dayroom. Kiesha walked in and flashes of her mom flooded her mind. Her mom picked out the curtains and wallpaper for the dayroom before she passed. It was the only thing that didn't change when her dad and Carmen got married and she redecorated.

"Have a seat Kiesha," Carmen said as she sat on the love seat with her.

"I know we haven't had the best relationship and I could never replace your mother, but I wanted to talk to you about your engagement to Roman. He seems to be nice enough, but I want you to be sure about marrying a man in this lifestyle. It's different when you're married to them than when you're dating. Powerful men can be very dismissive but it's because there are women that are willing to do anything to be with them. Like your friend, KK she hangs around and flaunts her affair in front of my face. I knew about it when she worked for the company and I let it go because I am here for the long run and all those other women are temporary. I am his backbone whether he recognizes it or not. When he gets older and is no use to the other women, I will be there to take care of him and give him what he needs."

"Wow, I never knew you felt this way about my father. I always assume that you were here for the money," said Kiesha.

"To be honest I started that way, but I grew to love him. I hated to see how women used him."

"We would be bankrupt if I didn't put a cap on the 'hoe card', " Carmen said.

"Hoe card," said Kiesha as she laughed.

"Yes, I had to get a separate credit card with a 100k credit limit just for dumb shit with these women. I have access to millions and they're only allowed 100k for the duration of their little flings," said Carmen.

"I guess it makes sense, but I want an old-fashioned relationship like my parents had before my dad became wealthy," Kiesha said.

"I completely understand," Carmen said.

"I wanted that, but your dad changed the rules and I evolved to meet his needs. I did the threesome thing; I joined the sex clubs, but nothing satisfied his appetite. I eventually found myself and my worth; I stood my ground."

"I didn't realize how much sacrifice it took to be with my dad," Kiesha said.

"It's a lot but I love him," she said as a tear fell from her eye.

"I want you to be sure that this is the lifestyle that you want to endure for the rest of your life," Carmen replied.

"I appreciate the concern," Kiesha said as she hugged Carmen.

"I know it's going to be hard but he's worth it," she whispered into Carmen's ear.

"Carmen and I had a little girl talk, everything is good."

"Wow," Roman and Noah said at the same time.

"I was wrong about Carmen," Kiesha said.
"She really loves you, dad."

"I'm glad to hear that," Noah said as he kissed Carmen on the forehead. Carmen was relieved that she was able to get through to Kiesha and maybe now her relationship with Noah will be better than it was before.

"When is the wedding?" Noah asked.

"We haven't decided on a date yet, but it will be a spring wedding," said Roman.

"I want to do it here at the estate," Kiesha said.

"I wish mom was here to see this."

"I am sure she is looking down," said Noah.

"Thanks dad," Kiesha said.

"I am going to hire a wedding planner because I know this is going to be a big job and I don't want to have the headache."

" I'll pay for the wedding, so spare no expenses," said Noah.

"Thanks dad," Kiesha said as she hopped up to hug her dad.

"Thanks, Noah," Roman said as he shook his hand.

"It's nothing I won't do for my daughter," Noah said as he puffed on his cigar. They all drank champagne and enjoyed the rest of the night.

Chapter 11

"Have those bricks been unloaded?" Roman asked, as he walked to his office of the warehouse.

"Yes," Quan said as he stacked the last brick in the drum that Roman seized from the Haitians.

"Great, you and the guys break that shit down. I'll have the whole east coast on lock when it's all done."

Quan and the guys worked hard to break down and package the product to get it out. "Quan, once you are finished, I want you to get all the heads together to inform them of the increase of product and the updated timeline. I am getting married. I don't have time to worry about this."

It was a warm day in April when the heads of the organization got together to agree upon the terms of the new shipment.

"Welcome ladies and gentlemen, we are here today to discuss the new terms of our agreement. I have recently acquired more products and I am speaking about an increase and influx of clients as well as money. I am offering a 35% increase in profit. Is this something you all would be interested in?"

Everyone said, "yes" in unison.

"If that's so I will have all the work delivered to you in the next day." Roman raised his glass to everyone they toasted and cheered.

"Quan can you make sure that everyone receives their package," Roman said once the room was cleared.

"We're going to be rolling in the dough soon boss," Quan said as he loaded the van.

"We sure will and I cannot wait to get back at those Haitian fuckers," said Roman.

" I hear you, boss," Quan responded. Quan hopped inside of the truck to make deliveries to the various heads.

&&&

Devereaux mansion

The dayroom was filled with sunflowers, candles, fabrics, lace, and cutlery waiting for the arrival of the wedding coordinator, Janise Colin. Janise pulled up to the estate and was impressed by the home and land.

"Wow, someone, who can afford me and doesn't have to worry about the cost," she said to herself as she exited her cherry red Aston Martin. Janise walked the stairs up to the great door and it was answered by an older gentleman. "How may I help you ma'am?" he asked.

"I am here to see Kiesha and Roman Case."

"Follow me," he said as he led her to the dayroom.

"Janise, I am so glad you were able to join us," Kiesha said as she reached her hand out to shake hers.

"It's an honor to be here," she said in response. Noah walked into the dayroom and Janise's eyes went straight to him, Kiesha cleared her throat.

"May we get started," Kiesha said to Janise.

"Of course, we shall," Janise said.

"I am thinking of a June wedding here at the estate. We can set up tents outside along with a dance floor. I want everything to be clean and colorful. We're thinking of the colors, lemon, and cream. I would like a sunflower centerpiece at all tables, lemon and cream tablecloths and clear colored plates and cutlery. I would like our last name to be on the dance floor and on the backdrop that is behind the bridal party table. Do you have any special requests dad or Carmen," Kiesha explained.

"No darling, it's whatever you would like on your special day," Carmen replied.

"I just want to make sure we have a nice father and daughter dance," Noah chimed in.

"Sounds great," said Janise. "I will get right on this; I will bill this to you later." There will not be a need for that. I am writing a check for 10 million and whatever is left over I want you to take it as a tip for such great service, I know you will provide," Noah said as he handed her the check and smiled at her.

Janise had always heard of the effect that Noah had on women, but she never experienced it firsthand and she must admit that everything they said was true. Noah was able to make you fall in love with just one look. Janise became moist as she touched his hand, his presence spoke volumes. "If nothing else I will get with you next week," said Janise.

Janise instantly called her best friend, Alyce on the phone. "Girl, you will never believe who I met today," Janise said as soon as her friend picked up the phone.

"Noah fucking Devereaux, the real estate mogul," she screamed.

"He was fucking gorgeous and his home is beautiful. His presence is so magnetic, and I fell under his spell."

"Damn girl," said Alyce. "You meet everyone planning weddings. I need to join you every once in a while to meet my next ex-husband honey," Alyce said jokely.

"I just wanted to check in right quick," Janise said as she hung up.

&&&

Roman

Roman looked down at his phone and saw Quan calling. "What's up to Q," he answered.

"All the deliveries had been made. I am headed back to park the van and then I am headed home, call me if anything happens."

"I will," Roman replied. He hung up and headed home to meet Kiesha. Roman parked and headed upstairs. The house was quiet, and it was odd for Kiesha to not have some sort of noise going. Roman crept inside of the bedroom to find Kiesha sleeping naked in the bed. Roman admired her beauty until he decided to join her in the bed. He dropped his shirt and trousers along with his underwear. His manhood sprung front, he kissed Kiesha on her neck and slightly on her breast.

Kiesha awakened and was temporarily stunned by him but was relieved when she saw Roman. She kissed him deeply and he slid his manhood inside of her and stroked long and slow. They both moaned and whimpered with every stroke. He climaxed and held her as they both fell asleep.

The sunlight coming through the windows peeped to let the couple know they made it to another day together.

"Good morning beautiful," Roman said to Kiesha.

"Good morning yourself handsome," Kiesha replied.

"I am going to meet Janise today, are you joining me?" Kiesha asked.

"I suppose I can squeeze in a little time to meet her."

"Great, let's get dressed and meet her at the café down the street."

"We have a ten o'clock meeting. Chop, chop, get dressed quickly," she said.

Roman and Kiesha got dressed and headed towards the café.

"Let's walk since it's such a beautiful day," Roman suggested.

They walked hand in and down Peachtree to the café. Janise was sitting at a table with her back towards the door when Kiesha and Roman walked inside of the café. "Janice," Kiesha said as she spotted her.

Janise stood up and smiled but her smile was quickly erased when she laid eyes on Roman.

"Janay?" Roman asked.

"It's Janise now Mr. Case."

"You both know each other Kiesha," said as she looked confused at the whole situation.

"Yes, this is my child's father," said Janise.

"I am not, our child died remember," Roman said.

"I do not have time for this foolishness today," said Roman as he put his shades on and headed back out of the door.

"What was that about?" Kiesha asked Janise.

"I was assured that you were a professional and you had no issue accepting the check my father wrote, I would hate to tell him he needs to stop payment on that check."

"That won't be necessary," said Janise.

"I assume the next time we meet you will not have an issue with my finance or I and not be reminded of your professionalism," said Kiesha.

"There will not be an issue ma'am, I do apologize," said Janise.

"Great," said Kiesha "we will meet you in a few days, I'll call you to let you know when," Kiesha said as she exited the café to join Roman.

"The nerve of that bitch," said Roman. "She really has the balls to bring up our deceased child, to do what? Make you jealous," Roman repiled.

"I'm so sorry, " said Roman.

"I don't want anything to come between us and our nuptials."

"I already knew about that; I never bring anyone around I haven't checked into. She does great work and that's why I hired her," said Kiesha.

"You are amazing," Roman said as he kissed Kiesha, they walked back to the penthouse hand in hand just as they had walked to the café. Roman was still fuming when they made it back home. "I cannot believe that bitch tried to pull that, and I can't believe that you knew who she was the entire time," he snickered to himself.

"I know that you are upset but she is the best wedding planner in the area and now she is planning our wedding."

"I am constantly surprised by you lately," he said while giving Kiesha the side-eye.

"I know," Kiesha said while kissing him on the forehead.

"I want our day to be perfect and no one is going to ruin it, not even a bitter ass woman who used to be your girlfriend."

"I can respect that," said Roman. He kissed Kiesha and headed out to work.

Chapter 12

Kiesha went into the room to get some extra cash out of the safe. Kiesha was stunned to see how much money was now in the safe. "Geesh," she said out loud.

"I guess that lick paid off," Kiesha said as she grabbed a million out and locked the safe back. She sent Roman a text about it as well. *Babe, I see our business venture paid off nicely.*

Kiesha grabbed her keys and headed out to Lenox Mall. She needed a little retail therapy between planning the wedding and killing those guys she needed a release. She went to Fendi and Louis Vuitton and a few more places before she called KK to meet her for lunch.

"Hey KK, what are you doing girl?" Kiesha said as KK picked up the phone.

"I'm not doing anything," said KK.

"Meet me at Lenox so we can go out for lunch," said Kiesha.

"Give me a half hour and I will be there," KK said as she disconnected. KK walked inside of the mall dressed head to toe in Fendi. Her hair was in a messy bun and face was beaten to the Gods. She looked amazing but felt horrible.

"Hey girl," KK said when she spotted Kiesha.

"Hey girl, you are looking amazing," Kiesha said. "Your face all did up on this good Tuesday."

"I had to make myself up because I feel bad for some reason, I think I got a little bug, or something," KK said.

"And you decided to bring that shit to me," Kiesha said while laughing but being very serious.

"I am not trying to get you sick; I know you are getting married soon honey. Let's hit the cheesecake factory and get a little something," KK said.

They were seated quickly, and both ordered herb crusted salmon.

"What has been going on with you?" KK asked.

"You know I am planning this wedding with Janise, the planner. Anyway, she tried to play me when Roman came with me to our meeting this morning," Kiesha replied.

"Bitch, what happened, " said KK.

"Roman and I walked into the restaurant and Janise turned around and noticed Roman and started going on about how she was his baby mother and all that jazz. Roman got instantly pissed but you know I put that bitch in her place. I hired her because she does great work I could careless about her fucking Roman years ago," Kiesha spatted.

"So, did she have a child with Roman?" asked KK.

"Their child died years ago, a couple hours after it was born so it wasn't like they had this amazing family or anything," Kiesha replied.

"I know you handled your business and it won't be an issue in the future," KK said as she laughed.

"Of course," Kiesha said as she raised a glass to celebrate with KK. "To us," she said as they clinked glasses.

"Excuse me," KK said as she got up from the table quickly. KK went to the bathroom and threw up, she put water on her face and rinsed her mouth when she finished. She came back to the table after she finished and left to go back home. Kiesha paid the tab for the two and headed towards Roman's office.

Kiesha let the top down on her convertible and enjoyed the Georgia sun, she was on top of the world. She was marrying the love of her life, she was rich, and beautiful. She played old school music and pressed the gas. She pulled up to the business and checked her lipstick in the car mirror before she got out. She walked inside of the building and noticed Roman had done some decorating in the lobby as well as new carpet. She nodded her head to the receptionist and sashayed to Roman's office. Kiesha lightly knocked on his office door before she entered.

"Hey Mrs. Case," Roman said as he stood up from his desk to hug Kiesha.

"How has your day been?" Kiesha asked.

"It has been pretty good; we have closed on three houses this week," said Roman.

"That's nice," she replied.

"We hardly get a chance to talk when we're home because it's always business," she said as she closed the blinds to his office.

"I like the upgrade to the lobby; I see the money is going to great use. How much did we make?" she asked.

"We did nicely," Roman said as he gave her a fist pump. "I think we should sell the high rise and get a home outside of the city. I think we should start on a family within the next five years also," she said.

"You have been thinking 'bout a lot," Roman said.

"Yes, I have so much has transpired in just a short period of time and I want to enjoy life with you and a little one."

"That sounds amazing baby," Roman said as he kissed Kiesha's shoulder.

"No baby I told you I am not having sex in your office again, last time everyone was looking at me crazy when I left."

"It's ok, this is my building and I do as I please."

"No," Kiesha giggled as Roman tugged at her skirt.

"Come on baby," Roman pleaded.

"Noooo," she giggled a little louder. Roman ran his hand up her skirt and tickled her insides.

"No," she said in a low whisper. Roman knew he had her where he wanted her. She opened her legs up and Roman kissed her on the cheek and told her, "alright ma'am I got things to do today." Then he patted her on the knee.

"What," Kiesha said as she opened her eyes.

"You said no and I respect that," Roman giggled. "You are a dirty mother fucker," Kiesha said as she laughed and grabbed her purse and left.

"I will see you tonight jackass," Kiesha said as she opened the office door and closed it. "Let me call KK and see if she's feeling better," Kiesha said out loud as she got back into her car.

"Call KK," she said to the car. "Calling KK," the car responded. The phone rang but KK never picked up.

Kiesha went home and fell asleep until she heard a loud noise. She hopped up and ran to the living room with her gun to find Roman and a few of his friend's downstairs playing pool.

"Oh, Miss lady," one of the gentlemen said as they noticed her with the heat.

"It's just us, " Roman said as he sipped his beer. "I didn't mean to wake you up, I am sorry."

"It's ok, I was about to get up anyway. You want me to order you guys some wings," she offered.

"That would be great," he said. Kiesha grabbed her keys and headed to the wing spot. Kiesha got the guys an assortment of wings and fries while she was out and headed back home. She gave the guys the food and headed back upstairs. She looked through the wedding magazine and wrote down more ideas. She couldn't believe she would be married next month. Her dress was almost finished from Ese Azenabor, she had one more meeting with Janise and everything would be complete. Roman joined Kiesha in bed around three o'clock that morning, she could smell the brandy on his breath and the cigar smoke on his clothes. He kissed Kiesha on her back and fell right to sleep.

&&&

Wedding Day...

The day finally arrived for Roman and Kiesha to become one. The Devereaux mansion was decorated with cream and apricot. There were submersible apricot colored orchids with floating candles and acrylic crystals that were the centerpiece of all the tables. The guests were dressed in all cream and mingled throughout the mansion. The dayroom was transformed into a cocktail waiting area. There was a cream-colored bar set on both sides of the room. The carpet was cream with a cream and apricot backdrop, there were flowers, and plants adorn all around the room. It was a mountain of seafood and a champagne fountain where guests could eat and drink before the nuptials began.

Noah and Carmen greeted everyone they could. Noah was dressed in a cream-colored Tom Ford suit and loafers. Carmen was dressed in a cream-colored cape Valentino dress with Valentino rock studded pumps. Her hair was pinned in a tight bun and her makeup was flawless. The staircase was draped with cream and apricot colored flowers. The cream carpet and cream and apricot colored background transformed the mansion into a wedding wonderland. Janise made her way through the home to make sure everything was in order. She contacted the bridal suite to see how things were going through her walkie talkie.

"I am so nervous," Kiesha said to KK.

"I have been waiting on this day for a while and now that it is here, I am shitting bricks."

"You will be fine," KK said to Kiesha.

"You guys have been through so much and today is the day that we celebrate your journey."

"I am ready to get this over with," Kiesha said.

"I am not used to all eyes being on me. My dad invited damn near the whole city out," Kiesha said while laughing nervously.

"I feel like it's my debutante coming out party again. I know part of being in society is having big parties, but this is a bit much. My dad has turned my wedding into his campaign kickoff for governor."

"You will be fine, Kiesha," KK said. "It's the nerves talking."

Kiesha looked in the mirror, her makeup and hair were finished, and she looked like a black queen. She became teary eyed when she saw her reflection, it was her mother's face looking back at her. She blotted her eyes with her handkerchief. Carmen walked into the room and tears fell from her face. "You look beautiful my daughter."

"Really," Kiesha said.

"Yes, you look beautiful, from the pictures I've seen of your mom, you look just like her. I have a gift I want to give to you," Carmen said.

"It's not much but it's a family heirloom, my mother gave it to me on my wedding day and I am giving it to you." Carmen opened a box and handed Kiesha a diamond crusted hair pin.

"My mother wore this on her wedding day as well as her mother and her mother before her. My family didn't have much but we have cherished this for generations."

"Thanks, it's beautiful and I will take great care of it." Carmen kissed Kiesha on the cheek and exited the room.

"That was sweet of her," said KK as she rolled her eyes as Carmen left the room.

"I didn't think you guys got along like that."

"We talked a few months ago and came to an understanding. She's a nice woman. I just never gave her a chance, " Kiesha said.

"That's nice I suppose," KK said skeptically. Kiesha stepped into her wedding dress and her breath was taken away by how beautiful she was.

"Roman is going to lose his mind when he sees me," Kiesha said.

"Yes, he is," KK replied. Janise entered the room. "Places everyone, it's almost time to get this show on the road. I need all the bride's maids lined up and ready to go. No gum or candy in your mouths ladies if you have any please spit it out now. Makeup please check everyone to make sure everyone is touched up and looking like perfection. Kiesha once all the ladies are lined up and headed down the aisle, I will be back for you to make your grand entrance. I am about to check on the groom's suite and I will be back."

Janise knocked on the door before she entered the groom's suite. "Gentlemen are you ready? I have the ladies lined up and ready to go."

"Give us a few minutes, we are all taking a last-minute shot to calm our nerves," one of the guys blurted out loud.

"Roman it has been an honor seeing you grow from a kid into the man you are now," said his Uncle Charles.

"I knew one day you would find someone great and settle down. Boy you've had enough pussy to last two lifetimes, and you live a life only a fourth of us will ever get to enjoy," he said already half tipsy.

"I love you like my own son and I wish you a lifetime of happiness, to Roman," Charles said as he raised his shot glass and drank his liquor quickly.

"All right boy let's get you married."

"OK, gentlemen can you please line up now with the ladies," said Janise. "Roman, you can make your way downstairs with your uncle Charles and we will get started."

Roman and Charles walked downstairs, and the orchestra began to play Canon in D. He smiled at the guest as he passed by and stood in front of the room by the pastor. The bridesmaids and Groomsmen walked down the stairs in rows of two. The ladies were dressed in apricot strapless chiffon gowns with a diamond midsection. The men were dressed in cream colored suits with apricot colored ties and vests. The orchestra continued to play until everyone was in their rightful place.

The wedding song began to play, and everyone stood on their feet. Kiesha took her first step and a unison of oohs and aahs came from the guest. Kiesha had on a full embroidered lace gown with a layered organza bottom and lace embroidered trim. She wore a pair of diamond encrusted chuck Taylor's under her dress because she wanted to be comfortable and no one would notice with the length of the dress. She walked down the stairs and the camera's flashed and she felt like a celebrity, all eyes were on her. When she reached the bottom of the steps her father was waiting for her.

"You look amazing pumpkin, just like your mom on our wedding day." He looked into her eyes and began to cry. Kiesha had never seen her father so emotional before. She got emotional as well.

"Stop dad," she said through clenched teeth as they made their way down the aisle. Noah was so proud to have Kiesha as his daughter, he raised her to have anything she wanted in life and now he was just to step back and let Roman take over. He wasn't thrilled about it, but he knew that was a part of his daughter becoming an adult. Noah shook Roman's hand. "Take care of my daughter," Noah said and he stepped aside and let Roman take his rightful place in Kiesha's life.

Kiesha and Roman exchanged vows in front of the city and her daddy announced his intentions of becoming mayor. The night was full of fun and laughter as the elite society of Georgia let their hair down and partied with the Devereaux's and Case family. Uncle Charles was the highlight of the reception for every young woman in a dress he just had to dance with.

Kiesha and Roman laughed at their uncle's shenanigans.

"Let's step away for a minute," Roman said to Kiesha.

"That's fine with me, we can go to my old bedroom." The two took the elevator to her room. Kiesha sat on the bed and took her shoes off. Roman loosened his tie and sat on the bed. He lifts Kiesha's feet on his lap and he began to massage them.

"That feels nice," she said.

"I am exhausted, all this show for one day," she said.

"Everything was beautiful and on time, I must admit Janise did a great job coordinating. I haven't seen her much," Roman said.

"Now that you mentioned it, I haven't seen her much since the beginning of the ceremony. I am sure she is somewhere being fabulous," said Kiesha. Roman kissed Kiesha, she knew they planned on waiting until their honeymoon, but she needed Roman at that very moment. She removed his tie and unbuttoned his shirt. She removed his shirt and jacket with one smooth motion.

"Damn girl," Roman said as he unbuttoned his pants and pulled down his boxers. Kiesha turned around so Roman could unzip her dress. "How in the world did you get into this dress?" Roman asked.

"Very carefully," she replied as she turned around with her bare breast showing and a thong.

"You look even better underneath all that," Roman said as he kissed her on the neck and shoulders.

Kiesha laid on the bed and removed her thongs and threw them at Roman.

"Come on Mr. Case," said Kiesha.

"I am on the way Mrs. Case," Roman said as he crawled to Kiesha on the bed. He slid into Kiesha and she cried out in ecstasy. He rocked in and out of her slowly and long. They developed a rhythm and were soon climaxing at the same time.

"Oh my God we have guests and I am sure they are wondering where we are." They both took a quick wash up and got dressed and then headed back downstairs. Kiesha and Roman decided to walk back downstairs instead of taking the elevator. Kiesha peeped in on her brother and noticed he was asleep in the bed. She didn't want to wake him, so she continued downstairs.

"Do you notice how quiet it has gotten," Roman said.

"Yes, I do," Kiesha replied.

"I wonder what is going on, I'm sure my father has some weird surprise going on," Kiesha said while laughing. Kiesha opened the door to the stairwell and stepped out. Janise grabbed Kiesha by the arm.

"Get out here bitch," she said as she pushed Kiesha onto a chair. "What the fuck are you doing," Roman said and a tall guy walked up from behind and pushed him onto a chair as well. Janise and the man had guns drawn on the couple.

"You think you were such a smart bitch, flaunting your money around and ordering me around like I was some sort of peasant. The whole time I was plotting on your bougie ass."

"Why are you doing this?" Roman asked. "If it's about money, we can pay you."

"Yes, it is about money 'bout a billion worth, isn't that how much you stole from my family when you killed my brother and his friends?"

"You don't have any brother's Janise," Roman said.

"Oh, yes, I do. After you and I split my mom got remarried. I think you may have known Louis Frantz; he kidnapped your bitch last year didn't he," Janise said.

"My father is Louis Frantz and my brother was Junior and I am willing to bet you had something to do with my missing brother and dead dad. Bring Noah's ass in here," Janise ordered.

"I was planning on getting you but when you called my office to plan your wedding you practically gave me yourself on a silver platter. I thought this was going to take months of planning but no you wanted a quick wedding and therefore I was able to do this quickly."

The guy brought Noah to the room. "Dad," Kiesha screamed out.

"I am ok," he said with blood pouring from his mouth and head. "Are you ok," he asked.

"I am fine." He was blindfolded so he had to take her word for it. Janise walked up to Noah and placed the gun to his head. "You took something from me and now I am taking something from you." Janise pulled the trigger and Noah's body instantly fell to the floor.

"No!" Kiesha and Roman screamed out at the same time. Kiesha screamed and cried and tried to charge at Janise but she pulled the gun on her to stop her. "Are you sure you want to do that princess," Janise asked. "Fuck you," Kiesha screamed out as she cried. "I can get you the money, just give me time," Roman said to Janise.

"Can you bring my brother or dad back," said Janise.

"You know I can't do that," he said to her.

"It seems like there isn't anything you can do for me then," she said.

"You motherfucking Devereaux's think you have Georgia on lock. What you thought you were going to Bonnie and Clyde some shit and nothing happens to you. I get it. You're crazy and in love with a Georgia Kingpin," Janise said while laughing.

The guy started laughing as well. "Your father raped me, did you think he was supposed to get away with it, " Kiesha said while spitting at Janise. Roman tried to tackle the guy again but he shot him in the stomach. Roman fell to the floor and held his stomach. He was bleeding profusely, "I'm sorry Kiesha," he said as he laid on the floor and life began to drain from his body.

"I never wanted this life to come back and haunt you. I love you with everything in me, remember that," he said as he closed his eyes and took his last breath. Kiesha was numb, she lost her mom, father, and now her husband.

"Just kill me already," Kiesha said to Janise. "Don't worry," said Janise. "It's coming."

Kiesha closed her eyes and continued to scream for Janise to kill her. Janise stood Kiesha up and shot her in the back of the head. Her body instantly hit the floor. "Is it finished yet," a voice said from the other room. "Yes, it is," Janise replied. Carmen walked into the room and stepped over Kiesha's body; she removed the hairpin from her hair. "Bitch," she said as she spit on Kiesha's body and walked out of the front door.

The End!!!